She Creatures of the Cass Corridor

Published in the United States by CreateSpace, a division of Amazon.com, Inc, Seattle
www.amazon.com
www.createspace.com

ISBN-13: 978-1469919744
ISBN-10: 1469919745

Printed in the United States of America

Cover Design by John Ryan

10 9 8 7 6 5 4 3 2 1

First Paperback Edition

Prologue

The party stores on Cass might as well have sold hookers, dope, and crack in aisle three. The street doesn't ask for identification. Brutally maimed, a wave of men began to turn up on the streets of murder city. Floods of girls disappeared in and around Wayne State University. A teen star was last seen at the ritzy Somerset Collection just north of Detroit. Lydia, an art teacher at WSU and the Center for Creative Studies did not like her children going out, even though their house was on Hancock, a safe and cozy street in the Woodbridge neighborhood just off campus. The recent pattern, violent even by Detroit's standards, did nothing to ease her fears for her children or the value of her home, which she had been trying to sell for nearly two years. When Lydia's daughter, the beautiful Alexandra, disappeared, she spiraled into her anxiety. The media gorged itself on the puzzle of the missing girls and mutilated men. The girls' faces couldn't be escaped. They were plastered on newsprint across the country. They became famous. The men, all murdered within a four-mile radius of the Cass Corridor, were deemed by the authorities to be upper-middle class johns looking for a good time.

Two of them were Tigers.

ONE

Lydia, her husband Victor, and Victor's brother John, moved to Detroit from New York City in 1985. There was more racial tension, more crime, more drugs, more of all the bad things every big city has, but seemed to be amplified thanks to the '67 Riots. John took a job teaching art history at WSU and welding at CCS. He got Lydia her job teaching ceramics and sculpture. He felt it was his responsibility. After all, who influenced Victor and Lydia to move out of New York? Victor made good money working in carpentry.

The three of them had grown up experimenting with drugs in the late 70's/early 80's New York post punk/art scene, but were known as 'chippers:' people who use hard drugs like heroin or cocaine on occasion, not habitually. For a while, John and Victor scored heroin on Fridays, two blocks from the university where John and Lydia taught. What none of them grasped completely was that for chippers, drug use was often more dangerous than to the seasoned addict. Chippers didn't understand how potent the drugs were, how to dose properly. They tended to overdose more often.

One Friday night, Lydia came home from work with some heroin that she was calling "mix-jive". John and Victor asked her why she kept calling it that. She told them the dealer called it that, said it was special. Anyways, it was all she could score. They shot it up. Victor shot up first. He was the strongest. He had the most experience. He'd know how much everyone else should do.

Lydia asked him what it was like.

"Uhhhh...I dunno...It, uh, feels kinda different, , uh, like some dope I once shot back in the...uh...Lower East Side, with Johnnnnnnny... Thundersssss, ya know, the guitarist for New York Dollzzzzzzz and Heart Breakerzzzzzz, man."

John and Lydia went for it. Lydia stood 5'7", a full-figured woman who could always keep up with the guys whether it was booze or junk. They got high, but worried about how strong the mix-jive was. Victor called Johnny Thunders. To John and Lydia's surprise, Johnny was not only home, he picked up the phone!

"You know those fluorescent lights that are like white tubes on the ceiling?"
In a frightened doped-out voice, Victor replied, "Yeah..."
"Well did you ever pop one and that white dusted vapor floated out?"
"That's what mix-jive is?"
"It's a mix of H and that white dust, the

Negroes seem to like it, but I wouldn't
fuck with it man. Why?

How you three holding up?

Did you just hit a bunch up

or something? Man, Wayne Kramer
used to tell me some wild stuff about
that shit, Detroit must be rockin' you
three, if you didn't miss, don't sweat it."
"Thanks Johnny. I'll call you soon. Bye."

Lydia looked blue. She was hardly
breathing. Victor and John took turns slapping
her and John threw water in her face. They
walked her around, and within a couple
minutes realized they'd have to take her to the
emergency room. Victor checked her pockets
and found her Valium script. He told the

doctors that the mix-jive/Valium combo was what did her in. They gave her a shot of narcon to negate the heroin. It woke her up and she was screaming, "Fuck! FUCK! FUUUUCK!" at the top of her lungs. She switched to pot, and only a joint every now and then. John stopped doing heroin, but he still gets wired on cocaine. He hides it okay enough.

TWO

Everything was getting better, but Detroit was still known by the special brand of crime that made it famous. Lydia wanted to go to the burbs, but the house wouldn't sell. Murder murder everywhere. Everything was getting worse.

Alexandra was changing. She befriended college girls, started dressing differently, wore more make-up and carried herself in a way she thought sophisticated adults carried themselves. She started smoking pot. Lydia worried that Alexandra would get involved with a local college boy, which was another reason she wanted out of the city. Too many hipsters, artists, and students. With all the incense and mineral spirits, Alexandra's room was practically a fire hazard. Lydia wanted her kids to grow up different.

Alexandra loved The White Stripes. She met them in a local diner, got their autographs. Whenever she would see them, her eyes lit up. There was a regional pride in liking The White Stripes. She met Terror at the Opera. Faith and Gretchen gave her hope that she could have a future in music that wasn't in 95.5's rotation. Faith played the accordion, but Alexandra wanted a keyboard. Her parents didn't want her to spend her birthday money buying some used synthesizer from a broke student named Tommy, but they couldn't stop

"Why won't you just let me express myself!? Maybe I don't want to paint anymore, okay?!"

They looked it up on Ebay and found that it normally goes for a grand. Lydia thinks Alexandra's getting it for $200 because Tommy's got a crush. Alexandra couldn't stop talking to Gretchen. Lydia and Victor didn't want to interfere, but music was kind of terrifying for them, especially because of the drug scene that sometimes goes along with it. Besides, they did the same things when they were her age. They didn't want to be hypocrites. John says Tommy's a good kid. Alexandra left to go get it at 7:00pm.

8:00pm: Nothing

9:00pm: Nothing

10:00pm: Nothing

10:22pm: Victor's yelling.

"What the hell is going on?!

Where is she?

I'm calling this Tommy boy right now!

Where is the goddamn number?"

"Next to the phone," Lydia muttered.

10:23pm: The phone rings. Victor picks it up. Lydia sighs in relief. The voice is male.

"Is Alexandra there?"

"Who's calling?"

"Tommy, Alexandra's friend with the keyboard."

"She left over 3 hours ago to buy that. It's not broken or anything, right?"

"No. Just a little used.

I was just calling because
I was going to go out and I was going to tell her that she can just get it from my roommate, J."

Victor asked, "Do you know where else she could be?"

"I don't know."

In an angry voice Victor demanded,
"Well,

where do you kids hang out?"

"In the day? Sometimes in the park..."

Victor explodes.

"You mean the park across the street
   from our fucking house?"
Tommy doesn't respond.

"Tommy?"
"Y-yes."
"She's a good-girl, you know that
   Tommy,

right?"

"Yes, Sir."

"If you see her, call me. I don't care what time it is."

"Sir, if, uh, I mean... when you find her, could you please have her call me too,

"Yeah." Victor hangs up the phone.

sir?"

The night was still, a moist fog began to linger. Lydia had never seen Victor so distraught. It was mid-April. The moon wasn't quite full, but it lit the sky. Detroit seemed warmer when the moon shone. Victor put his coat on. Lydia asked him where he was going. He was going to look in the park for

Alexandra. Her little brother, Jimmy, wanted to go with him, but he wouldn't let him.

"You're staying here with your mom."

Victor went into his tool room, pulled out his .38 Special, loaded it. Jimmy yelled.

"Mom! Dad! Come in here quick!"

Lydia and Victor rushed to Jimmy's room, overlooking the park. They only saw a navy Lincoln Town Car drive away.

Lydia asked, "Jimmy, what did you see?"
"I saw Alexandra walking through the

fog

very slow, so slow and scary,"

"Are you sure it was her!?" Lydia asked.

Jimmy shook his head.

"But she was wearing someone else's
clothes! She was wearing a mini-skirt.
Her eyes were really dark.

It happened really fast and there was
another person, but they were in the
fog

behind her. I didn't like it.

She talked to the guy in the car for a
second and then got in and left!"

Jimmy saw the same thing with another
girl a few months back. Victor and Lydia were
terrified. Trying to stay strong, for Lydia, and,
more importantly, for himself, Victor said,

"She probably just got drunk with friends and is too embarrassed to come home. Let's wait until morning before freaking out, okay?"

Lydia stayed to tuck Jimmy in for the night as Victor went downstairs and called John.

"I'm sure she's fine, Victor."
"I'm just worried she's on some crazy bender. She knows she can talk to us about this kind of thing."

"Yeah, like the time we told dad when we stole that briefcase

full of pills at Aunt Ellen's party when
you were 14, that was when
we spent the whole summer
on Placidyl and Quaaludes, right?
Kids experiment. It's normal.
Even if Alexandra comes home
hungover
and a bit strung out,
she's still your perfect little girl."

"Jimmy says he saw her at the park
across the street with some guy.
She got into a fucking town car and took
off dressed like a hooker,
John. How am I supposed to believe
she's just experimenting?"

John didn't respond.

"John? You there?"

"Yeah, yeah. I'm here. Didn't he see whatshername from Mexicantown wandering through the fog or something?"

"Margaret."

"Yeah. Didn't her parents come and talk to Jimmy about it?"

"Yeah. It was a few times. They showed him her picture and he just kept nodding that it was her. They came that last time though because he said he saw her again. I don't know, maybe I'm just freaking out. She's only been gone a few hours."

"What'd he tell her the second time?"

"Same thing he told us just now. Girl walking in the fog, strange man in the background, got into a car."

"What kind of car."

"Town car. Same as the one just now, but white."

"Seems like he's got a thing for those rides."

"We saw it take off, you fuck."

"And Alexandra was in it?"

"That's what Jimmy said."

"Jimmy says this. Jimmy says that. Victor, Jimmy's a bright kid, but I think he likes looking out that window too much. Remember Carlos Castenada staring off into the fog?"

"I'll talk to you tomorrow, John."

"Call me when she gets home."

"Will do."

Victor hung up the phone. The time was 1:15 A.M.

THREE

Victor filed a missing persons report when Alexandra didn't come home. The police came to the house and questioned Jimmy about what he saw. He told them exactly what he told Lydia and Victor. The cop asked Jimmy about the exact location of the mystery person. Jimmy, still dressed in his pajamas, stumbled on his words before settling on "the brush." The cop asked him if he could tell if Alexandra was aware of their presence.

"Yeah. He was right behind her. She had to have."

"So it was a he?"

"Definitely didn't look like a girl, sir."

"Can you tell me what he was wearing?"

"He was kind of shadowy. I can't say."

"So, Jimmy, I just want to make sure I got this right, your sister was not wearing her normal clothes. Right? A mini-skirt?"

"Yeah."

"And she had more makeup than usual, yeah?"

"Yes, sir. And she had black boots! Tall ones."

"So," the officer reiterated to Lydia and Victor, "let's get this straight. Alexandra went to buy an instrument off of a Thomas Arnold. Mr. Arnold has no idea of her whereabouts and she's been missing for less than twenty-four hours, which means we can't really do anything, but let me continue. Jimmy claims to have seen her standing across the street last night at around 11:30pm with a man behind her, acting as her shadow."

Jimmy jumped. "It looked like he was telling her what to say!"

Lydia became visibly anxious while Victor, arms crossed, tapped his foot. He wrapped his arm around her shoulder as the policeman began to speak.

"Ma'am, in the last year, five women have gone missing around that park. Three of them were spotted with a man described vaguely as 'a shadow.' He sometimes wears an overcoat, and is thought to have bad posture, but we're not entirely certain. We don't know what's going on, but we're working very hard. The trouble is that prostitution is like drugs. It's hard to catch and it all goes down before we even know anything. No one wants to go undercover anymore. Down on Cass, at the methadone clinic, we were looking for someone and the entire crowd started throwing dirty needles at us. One of our officers, poor guy had to get chemo. The needle that hit him was infected with HIV. We're just praying he doesn't get it."

Lydia, stunned, began to pine on all the reasons her daughter couldn't be turning tricks. The officer made a poor attempt to assure her that he didn't think that was the case before telling her they were just trying to look at the evidence from any possible angle. He confirmed the color of the town cars with Jimmy, and Lydia and Victor reminded the officer that they had seen the navy car as well, but that they didn't see Alexandra in it. They heard Jimmy scream, ran to his room and were told everything Jimmy had just recalled. His response was unenthusiastic.

"I don't mean to offend you ma'am, but are you certain Alexandra hasn't been using any drugs? Christ, we picked up a fifteen-year-old kid the other day for tricking. She was an all out junky. Either that girl was out of it, or she was purely in a daze. She didn't have I.D., wouldn't say a word. We still don't know who she is."

The cop asked Lydia if he could take a look at Alexandra's room. She obliged, and led him down the Berber-carpeted hallway to her door. The walls were covered with posters of David Bowie, The White Stripes, random cutouts and Daft Punk amongst others. Her vanity had black stripes of tape placed vertically across it, mimicking the cover of *Parallel Lines,* and the only uncovered space was the two inches surrounding her beloved poster for the Terror at the Opera show.

"What's Terror at the Opera?"
"Some band she was really into. They inspired her to go after that keyboard."
"We'll check into that, make sure she's not off on some rebellious rampage with some doomsy rock band."

It had been twenty-four hours since Alexandra had disappeared into the navy Town Car. Lydia was distraught, not just because their little girl was gone, but because they sold the house. They bought a new one in Birmingham. All the papers had been signed. They were moving in a week. She blamed herself for not moving fast enough in getting the hell out of Detroit. None of this would have happened. Alexandra wouldn't be getting into music, she wouldn't be getting into drugs, she wouldn't be wearing short skirts and smoky eyes getting into strange men's cars and Jimmy wouldn't be a total wreck. He was slumped on the floor in the corner of her room, just crying. Lydia sank down next to him and hugged him tight. "It's going to be okay. She's coming back."

Jimmy told her that they couldn't leave unless Alexandra came home. What if they left and she came back? Where would she go? Victor told him not to worry. Alexandra was coming home. Three days passed. Three heart wrenching, god-awful days. No one ate, no one packed, no one had the motivation to do anything.

"I'm going to miss this old house, even the squirrels in the walls."

Victor didn't care about the house. He cared about his daughter and he was starting to lose hope.

FOUR

Well kept and well made, their home had been built nearly a century ago by an eccentric mason. The walls were very thick. A passageway with no exit rested in the cellar. It was an attractive, lucrative piece of property, especially for Detroit, especially for somewhere outside of Indian Village or Boston Edison. It had been sold to an Ohioan chemist and his fiancée for $200,000. The chemist was to research cancer at the nearby Henry Ford Hospital. Victor held some respect for the man, but thought he was cold. Lydia just thought he had no soul. The kids were relatively indifferent, but held concerns of their own. How could someone so cold, so calculated, so scientific be able to settle into the warm, elegant, and bohemian space their parents had spent years creating? His name was Adam Harris.

John liked Adam enough, despite his family's misgivings. He even took him out to the pub for a couple of drinks one night. Adam was your standard classically handsome frat-boy, but much stiffer and nerdier than he appeared. Lydia thought he had a creepy smile that seemed like he had a deep guilty love for something perverse. She couldn't really put a finger on it, but, hey, he was the man buying their home. No one but him wanted it and she wanted out.

His reasons for wanting to move to Detroit seemed childish to Victor and Lydia. He had offers across the country, but chose Detroit for its music scene and low cost-of-living. These were some of the same things that drew John, Victor, and Lydia to the city, but, still, it seemed childish when he could be safer, and better paid on the East Coast. John was the only one who didn't think it weird, but he had a better memory of the past. He was the only one with a solid job all those years ago.

Morale remained low around the house as they took a couple extra days to get out of the house. They only ate because John brought them food. Victor and Lydia had taken a week off of work; Jimmy did the same for school. They didn't want to get up in the mornings. John took charge. He made them pack, and he was the one that convinced Jimmy to take time out from school to help. It didn't take long, once they got into the groove, even if they did turn into packing zombies, totally out-of-it, and constantly on the lookout for Alexandra. It was like they didn't know where they were going, what was going on, or who they were. All they knew was that they had to pack. Everyone was mentally asleep. Only John was awake. And he worried.

The new house cost $325,000. It was the cheapest one they could find on the outskirts of downtown Birmingham. Jimmy thought it was smaller, but there was actually more space. It had a finished basement with a wet-bar and an indoor whirlpool surrounded by mirrors. It was designed as a classy party space, but Lydia thought it was kind of tacky. John looked forward to spending evenings with Victor's liquor and the wet bar.

They packed like zombies, and so they settled like zombies, not giving much thought to furniture arrangement or general décor. John politely told them they all smelled like death, and so they washed up. It had been ten days since Alexandra had disappeared, and they had, against Jimmy's wishes, moved out of Woodbridge without her. John wasn't able to babysit them everyday anymore. Not only didn't he have the time, they were a good twenty minutes from him now. He could no longer be there at a moment's notice.

Jimmy knew about his father's gun, the .38 Special. He knew how to load it too. It was simple. Lydia and Victor lost hope for Alexandra's return, but Jimmy knew she was out there. He wouldn't give up hope. He knew he had to stay strong for his parents. John still showed up, just not every day like they were used to. He brought them groceries, even though they didn't eat, even though they didn't even use their refrigerator. He took Jimmy to McDonalds because he knew Jimmy would eat that, even if it was sacrificing nutrition. The kid had to eat. Victor and Lydia had moved, but they couldn't move. Jimmy was the only one of them outside of John who wasn't catatonic, who still believed Alexandra would waltz through that new door of theirs any minute.

FIVE

Jimmy shoved his dad's gun in his backpack and took a bus down into the city, getting off near his old neighborhood. He had to look for his sister, but all he saw were relatively clean-cut college students. He thought he saw Alexandra in a crowd, but when he ran up to her, it wasn't her. Her light brown hair flowed in the stiff, early spring breeze. While it wasn't winter, it wasn't exactly pretty weather to be wandering around looking for someone in. Jimmy's nose started running; he wiped the clear mucus on his sleeve. As he left campus, he felt he was getting closer to finding Alexandra, but it could have been that he was just getting closer to the streets he knew, closer to his old neighborhood. He reached the house he'd lived in a week ago. He rang the bell, and waited. No one opened the door. The breeze continued to assault his pale cheeks. Jimmy wiped his nose on his jacket sleeve a second time walking discontentedly down Trumbull Boulevard.

Jimmy cut through the parking lots of the low-income apartment buildings, and kept searching, even though he was beginning to feel that the trip was a wasted effort. He kept searching because his gut told him to keep looking. He was cold, and walking against the wind with his face down and his hands in his jean pockets. He was trying to keep a pace. He was trying to not let the world beat him. A girl wearing the exact same boots his sister had worn the night she disappeared stimulated his pre-pubescent mind.

She wore Alexandra's boots, black spandex, a pink short, a black mohair sweater, and a punky leather jacket. Jimmy ran up, but once he got to her, he had nothing to say. She just stared at him and then pushed him aside before moving on. He rummaged through his clouded mind, came to, and yanked the Polaroid of his sister he had in his pocket. He ran past her, turned around, and stopped in front of her.

"What?" she said.

"Hi, have you ever seen this girl? It's my sister."

She dazedly looked at the picture, not because she was confused, not because she was stoned, but not for any reason that Jimmy could understand. She walked on without giving him an answer. He stood there for a moment and began to cry. When she was a quarter of a block away, he wiped his eyes and yelled.

"Well!? Have you? This is important!"

A dark Town Car turned the corner. Jimmy edged his way back towards the low-income housing, where a young middle-class white kid like him clearly didn't belong, so he hid in a bush. The car lurked up to the girl. Jimmy couldn't see the driver, and he couldn't see the person the girl was talking to in the back seat. All he could hear was a deep voice telling her to get in. The car door opened, and as she was stepping in, about fifty yards away, a screaming figure came running from across Trumbull. The car door closed and drove off. The girl and the runner had disappeared.

Jimmy thought everything he just saw may have had something to do with his sister, but he couldn't piece it together. He committed himself to coming back to the city every Friday, riding between three different worlds, setting foot in two, and riding the Woodward bus back up to Birmingham by 8pm.

SIX

John and Lydia had not eaten or showered in a week. Their new home was falling apart. Both of them spent the days pulling out their hair and chewing on pencils. John was their only hope at survival. They kept repeating, "It ate our baby. It ate our baby." Jimmy went to school, but didn't talk much. He went into hiding. Everyone kept asking him about his sister. Before Alexandra went missing, she went to Roeper too. It was a bit of a hike before they moved, but Victor and Lydia sent them there because:

A) They didn't want their children being picked on for being the only white kids in class.

B) Lydia's uncle was a partial owner, which caused for a drastic drop in tuition.

And C) The school encouraged creative development.

It was Friday again. John came by with groceries and a more serious mood than normal. He insisted on talking to Lydia alone. They went to the den, which was as bare as the day they moved in and sat down on the floor against some boxes. He told her that the dean expected her back at work on Monday, but she just stared through him. He asked her if she could handle it. He asked her several times. He poked her and she snapped out of the daze. "Yeah, sure. Yeah."

"Good," he replied. "Now let's talk about setting this place up!"

Jimmy had told his parents the week before that he was going over to a classmate's house to work on a project for school, and he planned to do the same again today, but with the sunlight fading, he changed his plan and decided to go back into the city the following day. He'd put the pistol back where his father had been hiding it. Out of the entire house, Jimmy's room was the only one that made any kind of sense, and the only area in the new home that would remain making sense as his parents and uncle drank instead of getting the new house in order . He'd fallen asleep early, and woken up at 5 A.M. Uncle John was laying on the couch when he walked downstairs. He wasn't leaving yet.

"Can't sleep?" John asked.

Jimmy told him he'd just woken up and asked his uncle what he was watching. It was The Omega Man, an apocalyptic sci-fi from the early 70's starring Charlton Heston. Jimmy became engaged as his uncle fell asleep. The struggle between humanity and a diseased albino race that chooses to remain archaic as opposed to searching for a cure gave Jimmy newfound inspiration. He thought for a moment how he'd dodge everyone later and make it to the bus, then he tip-toed back to sleep and set his alarm for 11:30 A.M.

The alarm went off. It was set to his favorite radio station. A later Ramones song rang out as he pulled himself out from under the covers. "I want to live, I want to live my life," it sang. Jimmy got dressed, turned off the radio, and ran out the door. He didn't tell his parents where he was going. He didn't eat his cereal.

SEVEN

Adam Harris, the classically handsome university clone, was smoking a joint and cleaning his brand new house. The only thing that wasn't clonish about him was his height, which was almost five and a half feet. He was uncomfortable with his height to the point that he wore lifts in his designer shoes. A smart young man, his fiancée, Jen, a sweet, shapely woman with light brown eyes, was finally coming to see their future home. He fervently cleaned, trying to make it seem as inviting as possible. Unlike Victor and Lydia, Adam had no trouble settling in and the house looked completely different. Adam spent around fifteen grand giving it a more minimal look than the cluttered and cozy bohemia it was before. It didn't really matter, she was coming with the idea she'd already hate it, even if she was used to poorer cities. Detroit's different though. It was Detroit.

Adam had been efficient in his task. He'd started to prepare their dinner in advance of her arrival, a jet-lagged, romantic, candlelit evening for two starring a bottle of wine and homemade spaghetti. As he was chopping garlic for the sauce, he felt as if he was being watched, but concluded that the weed was just making him paranoid. He looked up at the clock. Jen's flight was scheduled to arrive in thirty minutes. He turned the oven to low so the sauce would stay warm, put on his pea coat, and ran out the door like a giddy schoolboy.

The kitchen was clean, the smell of garlic permeated the air. Some noises came from the wall across from the stove. It sounded like a squirrel in the wall, but it was going down. Finally, footsteps came up the stairs from the basement. A small black man. Dressed in many layers, mostly dark colors, a small head, he stands about 5'3", a peacefully dark look to his face. He makes a lot of noise when he walks, his clothing rubbing against itself, his rusty bones rubbing in arthritic agony. Casually, he walks into the kitchen, as if it were a place he feels at home, goes to the refrigerator, and helps himself to the two liter of Coca-Cola, gulping it from the container as if it were his, as if it was his house he was in.

The man goes to the stove, and reaches into his pockets, finding nothing. Reaching into one of his coat pockets, he pulls out a small salt-shaker and sprinkles white dust onto the back of his hand. He sniffs it and scrunches his face at its pungency. His alien black eyes and pin-prickly black pupils seem like they're producing some strange intoxicating tear in reaction to the powder.

He has a boyish glint in his eyes, but the whites have yellowed by decades of feeling lost, and liver failure. He looks at the leftover dust on the back of his hand and sinks into a daze. His hands were partially maimed, and he had scars from nearly a half century of shooting up, mostly heroin. One of the scars looked like an old mix-jive abscess caused by missing the vein. When the user misses, the fluoresce gets trapped under the skin and begins to agitate and infect, causing a collection of pus resulting in the rotting of flesh. The rotting tissue usually makes its way to the surface of the skin, causing an open sore. Abscess victims welcome maggots into their skin to eat the bacteria and infected dead flesh off. Although abscess scars usually signify IV use amongst old timer junkies from the late 60s to early 80s from mix-jive, abscesses are a norm for any IV user that graduates from hitting veins in their arms to legs, hands, genital areas, etc.

An abscess is just infected deteriorating flesh. On a hot summer day, you can smell a serious one from across a room. The man has a smell of rotten flesh and body odor feebly masked by CK-1 . Waking up out of his trance, he tosses the remaining dust over his left shoulder for good luck. Laughing to himself, smiling nonsensically at the ceiling, he maintains a look of intelligence. Then his mood aggressively changes, he angrily glares into the spaghetti sauce that he believes to have just called him a nigger. His eyes pop open and he starts shaking and shaking the powder into the sauce. He mixes it in with the wooden spoon on the side of the saucepan.

He tastes it and moans at its deliciousness before heading back down the stairs.

Beneath the stairs, he locates the crack where he fits behind the wall. He makes his way up the wall like a lizard and finds his tiny home on a moldy 2x4 from the early 1900s in front of the kitchen vent, high, near the ceiling. He comfortably sits as a child in a tree fort, where he anxiously waits for Adam and Jen to arrive. He falls into a deep nod, but is abruptly awakened by a knock. Knock. Knock. Knock.

Jimmy's eyes tear outside the door as, again, no one answers. There is a drip of clear snot hanging from his left nostril. He leaves, and the man goes back to sleep. Carrying Jen

and her suitcases through the threshold,
Adam beams once his fiancée compliments
him on how much she loves the house. He sets
her down, goes to the stove, tosses a few
remaining diced cloves of garlic into the sauce
and stirs. Adam and Jen go upstairs for a
quickie, then head back into the kitchen for
dinner.

"Ready to be fine dined my love," Adam
says in attempt to be suave.
"Definitely, my love!" she responds. "We
need some music!"

Jen heads over to the stack of CDs on the
counter and picks "Kind of Blue."

"Kind of Blue," she says to him.

As the first song starts to play, Adam starts serving; He sprinkles each plate with freshly ground parmesan from an expensive cheese grinder. Jen is impressed with Adam and, more importantly, with the house. As the first song plays on, the man in the wall slips into a daydream connected to the music, strolling down memory lane.

EIGHT

"Rufus! Rufus! There's a telegram here for you."

The 2x4 has disappeared, and in its place is a small bedroom and a saxophone stand. Rufus goes downstairs to read his message. "Miles Davis at The Cherokee Lounge Oct 19 STOP Invites Rufus Smith to sit in on tune." The telegram is from Miles Davis himself. His mother asks if Rufus knows who the man is. Rufus, very sarcastically replies in the affirmative. Of course he knows who Miles Davis is.

Two minutes later, the doorbell rings. Rufus' friends Tom and Joey are there. He

shows them the telegram with a note of
skepticism and asks them what they think
about it.

"Rufus, I was tellin' ya that Miles was at
that coffee shop when you did your solo,
even if he was just there to score some
dope off of Old Man Luke. He asked Luke
who you were and Luke gave him one of
your business cards. I told you those
were a good idea." Tom told him.
"But what if I go there with my sax and
it's a joke and Miles doesn't even want
me to play?"
"C'mon man," says Joey, "have some
confidence. You may be shy and a bit

square around the corners, but you blow that sax like the hippest cat in Detroit!"

"I second that and propose that the three of us dashing young men go out tonight in celebration. Celebration of what, you ask? The last night that our Rufus Smith was an undiscovered genius! C'mon Rufus," said Tom, slapping Rufus on the back as he stared at his feet, "What do ya say?"

"Fine," Rufus told them.

"Then it's settled! First we'll go to the malt shop and tell everyone, then we'll get some doll food–"

Rufus interrupted Tom. "Doll food?"

"Heroin, let me finish. So then we'll go to Old Man Luke and score some dope and

then we'll go to my cousin's whore
house and then we'll go to the bathroom
and get zooted and then –"
Rufus interrupted him again. "And then
I'll get busted by Charlene."
"I'll take care of that."
"Yeah, Rufus," Joey butted in, "In fact,
don't even tell Charlene you're playing
tomorrow. Make it a surprise."
"We know what we're doing, guy. After
all, who helped you get her as a
girlfriend in the first place? And then, as
I was saying, we'll get all zooted and
we'll do our thing with my cousin's
ladies. We'll screw 'em all night long.
Cause we'll be zooted. Ha!"

"We can screw them all night?" Joey asked.

"Well, for an hour."

So the three guys walked to the malt shop. It was a black working-class neighborhood, and while the kids that the boys hung out with were the smarter, more cultured kids, it was starting to be hip to inject heroin, sniff cocaine, and smoke reefer. Some of their friends hadn't made it through high school. Some of their friends were in prison. Some of their friends were hustlers. Some of their friends were going to University of Detroit on basketball scholarships. Some of their friends were already dead.

Tom, Joey, and Rufus were well respected in all circles, known as the smarter, hipper cats who walked the line, but never ended up on the wrong side. Rufus saw his girlfriend, Charlene. Rufus was very shy. Charlene was very loving. Rufus said very little and just sipped at his shake. The boys were mingling with the other boys and girls at the malt shop. The average age was twenty, and it was mostly black kids that went to U of D and Wayne State, that were an extreme minority to both school's student populous.

"Okay. Gotta go, c'mon Rufus, bye Charlene." Tom says abruptly.

They dragged him out of the malt shop and headed to the Cass Corridor. Rufus seemed nervous. He asked Tommy if he had his blade. Tom flashed the switchblade, which made Rufus feel at ease. The hookers, degenerates, and hustlers started to become apparent, as if the boys had some kind of lunar, nocturnal night-vision. They saw this girl that they all used to have a crush on, Rachel, and she didn't look so good. Her face showed the experience of multiple rapes, coat-hanger abortions, and bad junk. She stared at them like a vicious dog protecting it's T-bone steak, watching every step they took as they marched on. Her stare gave them a 'clean inexperienced/out-of-their-league' feel, which was fine. They didn't want to be in her league.

They didn't even want to mention it. They walked up to a doorway in a back alley that smelled like sewage. They knocked.

"Password," a deep voice said from the other side.

"C'mon, man. It's Tom!"

"Password," the voice said louder

"Fine. Here kitty kitty kitty pretty kitty."

The door opened, creaking louder than the door at Castle Dracula. The boys walked in, a beaten-up dog barked. Old Man Luke told the dog, Sparky, to shut up. The dog obeyed, and sat down in the corner of the kitchen that smelled like old grease and mildew. The Dickensian Old Man Luke wore an old German military surplus coat. World War One. He was missing a leg, but no one was really certain if he had been in the war. Many were skeptical, but gave him the benefit of the doubt since he was missing a leg. He said the Germans blew it off. There was proof, though, in a Purple Heart medal he had on his mantle in a display case. The boys had known him since they were small, and he used to let him knock on his wooden leg for good luck.

"So what brings you to my neck of the woods boys?" Luke asked them.

"We need some H." Tom said.

"Well boys, normally you'd be in luck, cause I know you just want a kick and you're not gonna get addicted like your

Old Uncle Luke, but I'm sorry the H I have is just too strong, and I don't want to send you boys to your grave."

"C'mon Luke," Joey pleaded, "Rufus has a big show with Miles Davis, tomorrow."

"Who the fuck is that? Besides, I'm supposed to let you guys kill yourselves so Rufus can't play a show?"

"He's a jazz musician,," Tom said, "He bought dope off you. You gave him one of Rufus' cards. Don't you remember?"

"Oh, yeah, that little guy, real serious. Is that what you're going to do now, Rufus? Be a dope addicted jazz man?"

"Wait," Rufus replied, " Luke. You're worried about us overdosing, yeah? So how about if we just do a little here with you and you can see for yourself that we'll be okay, and if it's too heavy, we'll just chill with you until it wears off." "If you guys give me a couple extra bucks, because it's so good, and you're making me babysit, then I'll do it."

The boys pulled their money out and gave him ten bucks, which was enough for the three of them to stay high all night. Tom pulled a fresh syringe out of his pocket. It was the only thing in the house that shined. People said that Old Luke didn't have electricity, but he used the radio and once in a while, he'd play some big band stuff or Beethoven on his old phonograph. The reason they said he didn't have electricity was because of the candles. There were ten candlesticks, gobs of solid wax dripping from their bases. Luke was obsessed with arranging knick-knacks and candles in a certain way. He had the religious intensity of a Roman priest, sharpening an old German syringe on a fine grinding stone. Not many people saw or believed that he used some special German syringe. He said that this was the exact kind that Hitler used for his daily injection of morphine, meth-amphetamines and vitamins.

Old Luke always told the boys that he doesn't get high with people he doesn't trust, then go on to give some kind of reason to justify his junkieness. According to Luke, it started during the war, the government gave him morphine, and he still receives disability checks, the only thing that keeps him going. Just when other people succumbed to more criminal ways of getting their fix, Luke would just get a check, and wisely invest in dope deals. He was lucky to have people's respect and acceptance even though he was a junkie. It was easier accepting his reasoning over someone just wanting a kick.

Luke was a real character, a living piece of junk art, and a living contradiction. The leg being blown off by Germans, the being half-German, and the German syringe all caused the boys to call Old Luke "The German Nigger." Old Luke didn't allow the N-Word in his home. Fearing and loving the prick of the needle, everyone got high. The boys shared

Tom's syringe. Rufus ran to the bathroom and vomited. Tom was right behind him. Joey sat, silently watching the giant shadow flicker against the wall in a giant dichotomous monster-nightmare/opiate dream.

"Joey," Luke said, "You're very quiet tonight."
"What?"

Luke didn't reply, he was totally fucked up. He wasn't bullshitting the boys about how pure the dope was. They could have stayed all night, but Joey snapped and told the boys they had to roll.

"Can we have the rest of our dope,

Luke?"

"What?" Luke said, waking up from his

Tom asked.

daze, "Oh, yeah, yeah. It's your dope.

Take it." He walked into his bedroom.

The boys thanked him and left. They were back in the wasteland, about a mile left to walk. A taxi came, but wouldn't stop. They had walked out of the worst part of town towards the university. Tom's cousin ran a prostitution ring, in the Sutton Homes Apartments. The boys ended up getting a ride from one of Joey's sister's friends. Everyone said this guy Jake was gay, but the boys didn't care, especially since he had wheels. He told them that the neighborhood was getting more dangerous by the day.

"Yeah," Joey snarled, "For whores, johns and junkies."

"Well that's what you guys are, right?"

"What's that supposed to mean?" Rufus asked.

"Well, you guys are either out here scoring dope, or getting pussy, right Rufus?"

"Yeah. That's about it."

"Did someone tell you something?" Tom asked Jake.

Jake smiled and said, making his voice a tad more fey than usual, "All serious jazz musicians do narcotics. Hell, jazz is a narcotic, and besides, every jazz cat dreams to blow the horn like Charlie Parker."

Jake laughed an effeminate laugh, which startled the boys. Joey told him to stop. Jake slammed his foot on the brakes and everyone except him lurched forward. Rufus thanked Jake for the ride. He was the only one who said goodbye on the way out of the car.

NINE

Charlene is still in the malt shop. Mary Lou Johnson and Sara Roberts, two catty girls that Tom and Joey are always trying to impress, stop her on her way out. Mary Lou is half-white, with freckles. She claims to have slept with Charlie Parker and Miles Davis. Sara Roberts is a slender girl with similar complexion to Mary Lou, who's snobby about her education and affinity for jazz. She has a thing for Rufus.

"See you tomorrow at The Cherokee, Charlene." They say to her in unison.
"What?"

"You don't know?" Mary Lou says, smiling, "Miles is playing with your man at The

Cherokee tomorrow."

Charlene frowns and runs out of the malt shop, tears streaming from her eyes. Mary Lou and Sara are laughing from the inside. Charlene wants to kill someone, only she's not exactly sure who. She's narrowed it down to those girls or Rufus or Tom and Joey. Walking home, her rage grows as her mind searches for an answer to what exactly it was that Rufus and the boys had up their sleeves. She loved him and worried about losing him to his friends, or, more likely, to his music. She worried constantly.

Usually Charlene was well composed and overly logical, but now? Now she was walking home in a desperate fit, tears and snot running down her face. A tall, thin woman dressed in gray wool bumped into her while leaving the fortuneteller's shop. She wore expensive gloves and had the look of a sophisticate.

"Young lady," she said to Charlene, "are you okay?"

"I don't know," the tears kept gushing, and it was hard to understand her.

"What' the problem?"

"Boy trouble."

"Boys are trouble, no need to beat

yourself up over them though."

Charlene smiled, as the woman pulled a handkerchief from her pocket book.

"Here," she said, "Let me wipe that mess off your face. It's okay, a man can always mess a fine lady such as yourself up, but you, you can always mess him up twice as bad! Why don't you come inside?"

"I must be going."

"To find that man and mess him up? You want to know what he's doing?"

"Well, yeah."

"Come inside."

"I barely have any money."

"On the house. It's been a good night. Some rich women from Dearborn came and we held a séance."

"Maybe I shouldn't–"

"Nonsense! Are you afraid this might be oohh" the woman said in a sarcastically menacing tone, "dabbling in the black arts?"

"A little."

"The magic I work in is of the light. When I do something of the dark, it is to counteract the black. Do you understand?"

"No."

"My name's Raquel, Charlene. Come in."

"Wait, how did you know my name was Charlene?"

"Charlene is such a pretty name, and you're such a pretty girl to go along with it. Pretty girls shouldn't be crying like this. Inside. Tell me the problem as we go."

They walked in the house. Charlene told her up the steps and on the way in about Rufus, about his gig with Miles Davis, about him not telling her about it, about the other girls knowing. Raquel suggests that maybe he just wanted to surprise her. Charlene thinks his friends are just up to something. Raquel goes into the backroom for a moment, while Charlene waits outside. In the backroom, Raquel rolls white powder and a mudded clay substance into a ball. She lights the coals of a blue hookah and drops the ball on the coals, inhaling the whole thing in two drags. The smoke smells very sweet. It feels like incense. Raquel's eyes get teary as she floats back into the other room. Charlene thinks that it is all a show, but is scared. Raquel senses her fear and assures her that she is to have no worry.

On the table in front of Raquel is a machine, which appears to be a scale. Raquel pours oil into it. The oil drips out almost immediately, a mechanical fountain. Charlene thought she might have an idea of what the device might be. She remembers reading a book describing a similar device with which Nostradamus made his predictions in a medicated state. Raquel was definitely medicated, but she always thought of these things as myth, fantasy. Here it was, though, with Raquel staring deeply into it. All the machine did was drip droplets of oil into a miniature pool of more oil, causing ripples. It dripped at a slow but yet methodic pace. With each drop the atmosphere of the room seemed to change, although it looked the same. Raquel's voice changed as well. What was once friendly and light was now serious and deep.

"What is his full name?"

"Rufus Smith."

"What is his date of birth?"

"March 4, 1938"

"Give me your hand and visualize him"

As Charlene began to extend her hand, without any effort her hand immediately magnetically linked together with Raquel's hand. As Charlene felt a surge run from her hand to the rest of her body, she felt a unity, an almost unexplainable oneness with Racquel.

Unearthly!

In a lucid, monotone, unenthused voice "Yes, I see him. He is being led into a room by a woman of the night. She is taking off her clothes? Need I go on? "Yes!" Charlene screams while crying.

Raquel has transformed into something not of this world, her shadow casting up the wall, a black-magic Occult monstrosity. In a loose tone, she proclaims, "The girl washes her filthy cunt. She's taking Rufus' pants off. He tries to kiss her. She won't let him. She is now performing fellatio. They are copulating!"

"No!" Charlene cries.

"Yes!"

"No! You're lying!" she says as more tears flood her face.

Raquel snaps from the trance, but remains medicated. Coming to her senses, she tells Charlene that, difficult as it may be, it's the truth, and that Charlene knows the truth, that she knew something bad was going to happen. Charlene relaxes, stops hyperventilating. Raquel tells her she'll be okay, but Charlene doesn't believe it. She still wants Rufus, and she wants Raquel to get him back for her.

"No, a young fresh girl like you getting her hands dirtied by the dark arts? I won't have it."

"Please, I beg you!"

Raquel has stopped paying attention, and is sifting through her mail. Opening one envelope, she exclaims "Shit!" Charlene cranes her neck so she can see the letter. It's a bill.

"I'll give you twenty bucks," she says.

"Fine. What do you want to
do with him?
You want him to come back?"
"No, I know he'll come back to me."
"That's life, honey. Men are dogs, and
you're just going to have to get used to
it. And musicians? Ha! The worst of the
lot!"
"I want to mess his show up tomorrow. I
want to make it so he can't play."
"Would you like me to make a voodoo
doll out of him?" she asked, holding out
her hand, waiting for the twenty, "Then
you can just do what you want with
him."

"Yes," Charlene said, smiling, and passing the note, "I would like that very much.

The shadows of the two women resembled witches at a black mass. The next day, Rufus called Charlene, and told her he had a surprise, but she already knew. She told him she knew and that she wasn't interested. Rufus begged Charlene. She wouldn't go. He begged her some more. She said she'd meet him there. He warmed up all day long, but was unusually loose, dizzy from a night of hard dope and cheap women. Making friends with the dizziness and the after-life of the heroin, he became less nervous. He took a nap, and woke up half an hour before show time. He would have missed it if some college kid named Barry who lived next door hadn't driven him. Barry was a big jazz fan. He felt honored to drive Rufus.

They got to the club, and there was a huge crowd. Everyone looked at Rufus with respect.

James smiled at him, and said " Yeah, Rufus. Jazz is the future. You're on board!"

Rufus went to the bathroom, set down his saxophone, and took a long relaxing piss. His arms cramped up. Suddenly it wasn't so relaxing. They felt like they were shrinking, or getting pushed into his body. He couldn't zip his pants back up. His arms were hurting more and more. He motioned to the front door to get some fresh air. He started screaming. The crowd grew silent. He was screaming like a girl in agony which morphed into a putrid newborn's throat being slit, gurgling sound . Tommy tried helping him. Rufus seemed like he was about to combust, as he made his way out the building. Pausing for a breath and realizing he was still holding his sax. He made a long extended caveman grunt and threw his saxophone against the brick wall in the alley. He threw it at such a speed that no one could see it flying through the air. They just heard the loud, destructive sound of a saxophone being smashed against a brick wall and the sounds of the hundred pieces of sax shrapnel that shot all around and realized that it had came from Rufus's hand. Rufus then ran in wide strides, in a goof-like manner. He ran in a straight line and didn't stop for cars. He had completely disappeared within a half minute. Those who knew Rufus realized that Rufus would be gone forever.

Charlene died of a heroin overdose in France, in March of 1962. March 4th Rufus's birthday.

TEN

A glass hits the floor of Adam's kitchen, breaking. Old Rufus wakes from his reflective, self-actualizing flashback daydream. He opens his eyes, and sees Adam passed out with his face leaning against the white tablecloth. Jen's face is in the spaghetti. Rufus smiles and pulls out his cheap 'blow-out' cell phone. He dials a number.

"Dusty, I've got the new guy's girl. Why don't you come on down? Yeah, come to the back door. I'll be waiting for you."

Rufus slinks down the wall, and back up the basement stairs. His hands are in his pants, and he has a great big smile on his face.

Rufus heads straight to Jen, unbuttoning her shirt. He pulls a small switchblade from his pocket, popping its trigger. The blade flicks out clumsily and slowly. The blade is sharp, but the handle was dulled, off-white mother-of-pearl. He slices Jen's bra in half at the center from the front. Her nipples are rosy and have a gelatinous bounce. Jen was proud of her bosom, and now? So was Rufus.

He was breathing very deeply, and unnaturally, drooling, forgetting how to behave. He rocks back and forth. Kneeling down, he sucks on Jen's nipples, her leg between his. He humps her. Adam snores. He moves. Rufus, spooked, realizes he only has so much time before they awake. He looks at the boom box on the countertop, and listens to Miles for a second. Miles' "On the Corner" is also on the countertop. He steals "Kind of Blue" and puts "On the Corner" on, with a childish smile on his face. A knock at the door, a person who looks deformed. Black, but light skinned, pretty face, girlish, messed up posture, a ghetto Hunchback of Notre Dame.

Rufus points towards the kitchen, letting the hunchback go first. He grabs Jen, drags her out back to the baby blue minivan in the alley. She's thrown in on top of a pair of beanbags, a sleeping bag laid over her. Dusty drives. Rufus is in the back of the car, caressing Jen's perky nipples. He's rocking back and forth again, breathing loudly, off pattern. Sucking, biting, humping, jiggling. Rufus only comes up to her shoulder, a little kid taking advantage of his babysitter.

Jen smiles , orgasms. Rufus humps her harder. "Take that bitch!"

Still in half slumber, but annoyed at her discomfort, Jen grabs Rufus' face and says Adam's name. Adam. Adam. Adam. She opens her eyes to understand what's going on. Rufus gives her a stupid grin, and keeps humping. Jen yells at him to stop. He keeps humping. Jen kicks him off her with her free leg.

"Oh c'mon, girl. I'm gonna have you whether you like me or not, so you've got the chance to be in control. You can love Rufus, or Rufus can make you love Rufus."

"Shit!" Dusty says from the front, "The girls are almost home."

The time is eight o'clock. It's night. They get home, and pull into a house, a few blocks from Grand River Avenue and Warren. Their house is a pre-war two-story home. It's a little run-down, but Rufus has Dusty take care of it. The Formica kitchen is complete with a small stove and stainless steel refrigerator. The family and dining rooms have parquet floors.

The kitchen and bathrooms, marble. The upstairs, white shag carpeting. Pristine. The drapes are red velvet. They have a large plasma television, hundreds of classic movies. There's mostly horror and science fiction. Very B-List. One wall is full of VHS. One wall is full of DVDs. One wall is full of CDs. One wall is full of books, many books, books on the occult, books dating back to the early 18th century. There's a side entrance to the house. Dusty pulls the van up to it.

They drag Jen's limp, semi-conscious body into the house and down the stairs into a white dungeon. Everything is painted white with very thick paint. Everything looks very clean. 20 army cots lay in regimented order.

They lay Jen down on a cot in the back. The door upstairs open, down comes a line of hauntingly beautiful young women, a fashion show for the damned and vagrant, marching in strict formation, thematically linked by the colors of pink, purple, lime, and gray. They're dressed in a sexy streetwise manner. They're dressed in both designer and secondhand. Everyone is wearing a lot of eye shadow and mascara, to match the outfits, rosy cheeks, and deep lipstick. They stop, still in a line.

Dusty grabs a large, clear, sleek pitcher filled with blue from the refrigerator in the basement. One of the girls steps out of line, and grabs a stack of Dixie Cups, passing one to each girl, where they stand at attention, holding the cups as if they were to receive communion. The girls are in an attentive trance. They wouldn't participate if they were in their right minds. Dusty motions for each model to approach their bed and drink the fluid, one by one. He catches and tucks them in as they pass out from the potion.

After all the girls are tucked in, he gets out his tackle-box of makeup, and grabs his stool. He walks up to the first girl, sets down his stool, and combs her long, beautiful hair worthy of a show horse. After grabbing a bucket and a sponge, he gives each girl her daily sponge bath, precise and methodic in his duties. When their faces are dry, and the day's makeup has been cleaned, he applies fresh makeup with finesse, each move more meticulous than the last. Dusty takes pride in his work. He's a real pro, and he loves the girls. Who'd take care of them if he didn't? Someone else? They'd work for someone else? No.

He felt they had to look as beautiful as possible in order to make their victims more comfortable with the concept of their death. Rufus put the idea into Dusty's head and Dusty made it ritual, made it complex. It's their pretty little faces that they see before dying, before burning in hell. Rufus liked to say prostitution was disgusting. Dusty had ideas, but he wasn't really capable of rational thought, only excelling at certain things (driving, makeup, hygiene) due to his autism. He doesn't challenge Rufus because he's happy enough being with the girls. He tells Rufus he is in love with Desaray. Rufus smacks him with a black jack.

The girls always go to bed at 8:15 P.M and they always wake up just over four hours later. Half of the girls are sent to the hard east side. Half of the girls are sent to the Cass Corridor and its surroundings.

ELEVEN

Adam woke up to find no Jen, a broken
wine glass on the floor, and the wrong Miles
Davis album playing. Miles wails frantically on
the trumpet, summoning his demons both
noisy and avant-garde. This was Jen's least
favorite Davis. Why was it playing? He
couldn't remember. His memory was foggy.
The spaghetti was great and then? Nothing.
Screaming Jen's name Adam runs through the
house. She doesn't answer. Something's
happened. He begins to cry before composing
himself enough to call the police. Two hours
go by, no cops. Sheer terror. Adam takes the
vigilantly justice route. He doesn't have a gun,
but he has mace, which he has a firm, sweaty

grip on. Adam puts on his pea coat and runs out the door.

John is at a party store, the seediest one in town, near a bunch of hotels and apartments that the fiends hang out in. When he walks in, a black man in a baby blue, velour jogging suit asks him what he needs. John pauses for a moment, feeling nervous. Looking at the Arabic man at the counter, he tells the man he needs nothing.

"Oh, c'mon man, you need something!
Whatever it is you need, I can get?
Yayo?
Smack? Weed? Women? I got it.
What do you say?"

John purchases a bottle of Southern Comfort, and leaves. The man in the jogging suit follows him.

"C'mon man! The women are young, beautiful white girls. Huh? C'mon."

"You a cop?" John asks him.

"No I aint no cop!"

"How much for a fuck?"

"Fifty," he whispers

"Yeah?"

"Follow me."

John paused for a moment.

"You coming or not?" the man asked.

"How far is it?"

"Just a block."

They walk up to the King's Arms on the avenue. He spotted John's weakness: easy sex. John was a sucker for teenaged white hookers. He walked into the hotel. An older black man held court in amber-tinted Italian sunglasses. The man in the jogging suit told the concierge that John was with him and they went up a flight of stairs. The hotel was cramped, with a soapy, used, soggy smell to it. The hallways reeked. The sound of televisions and moaning filled the space.

"Here it is, man. 210. She'll be here in a second. You'll like her. Cornbread fed. Ohio."

John walks in. The room isn't filthy. It's not clean, but it's not filthy. He plops himself on the bed, bouncing a little bit. The door opens. A tall, slender, sexy silhouette stands in the doorway.

TWELVE

"Come in. Close the door."

The girl walks into the light. John can't believe it. It's Alexandra. He runs to her, hugs her. She grabs his hand and places it onto her breast.

"Alexandra! It's me! Uncle John. Don't you recognize me?"

She pulls out a double-edged dagger to stab him, but he catches her arm. The door bursts open. The man in the jogging suit runs at him like a wild panther. John crouches down and flips the guy over his back, and through the window. Two seconds. Smack.

Rattle. John looks out the window. The man is dead and bloodied. A little kid looks up, but he can't make out John. Alexandra runs out of the hotel and onto the street. John follows her. Bums and crack heads surround the body. They're picking him for drugs and money. John walks a little more casually until he passes them. Alexandra is walking fast up Second.

"Alexandra! Alexandra!" John yells.

She's running. She's running fast. John is only about forty feet behind her. A baby-blue minivan going seventy swoops up behind him. John misses death by mere inches. He jumps. Alexandra glances at him as if her mind and spirit had been taken over by an army of whores and witches. Coldly, she shrugs at him, gets in the van, and disappears.

"Alexandra!"

It's no use. John thought about what to do. He didn't know. He didn't want anyone to know what Alexandra had gotten herself into. Something bigger was at play here, something more complex than his niece getting kidnapped or his niece turning to a life of prostitution. Nothing made sense. He knew she'd been taken over by something. It was beyond addiction. That was Alexandra's body, but it wasn't Alexandra. Why had she run to the streets and left everything behind?

He went home, just after 5:30 AM, exhausted, needing sleep. Jimmy was sitting on his porch, arms crossed, shaking freezing to death.

"What the hell are you doing here?" John said lifting Jimmy up.

"I was looking for Alexandra?"

"So you need a place to crash?"

"Yeah."

"Couch is all yours, guy."

He set some blankets and a pillow on the couch. They fell asleep instantly, worn out from their bereavements. The next day, John woke just before two. He went downstairs, not fully believing the events of the previous night. It wasn't real, had to have just been some terrible nightmare. The blanket he tucked Jimmy in was loosely folded, the pillow set atop. Jimmy had taken off. He knew he was out looking for Alexandra. He didn't want to tell Victor and Lydia, but he knew he had to.

"Lydia, uh, Jimmy spent last night here."

"Good, let me talk to him."

"He, uh, left before I woke up."

"He what? Where did he go?" she screamed through the telephone.

"I don't know. I know he'll be back though."

"How did he even get down there?"

"I don't know. The bus? I've got to scoot, but I'll leave the door unlocked for Jimmy and a note to tell him to call you."

Lydia was upset, but relieved her son wasn't dead. John started trying to piece together what happened. The only person he thought might be able to give him some information was the guy who owned that party store he met that pimp at. He carried a gun identical to Victor's, a .38 Special, snub nose, always loaded. John loaded it with bullets that had hollow points. He walked to the store. The sky was gray; the sun peeked out, an airplane buzzed through the sky. The guy from last night wasn't there. It was a

younger guy, but still Arabic, who gave him a
strange look. Two men argued in Kurdish. The
man at the counter placed a phone call as John
walked in. The arguers saw him and stopped
arguing. John knew something was wrong. He
grabbed a liter of coke. The owner, the man
from the night before, walked in from the
back. John asked him for a bottle of Jack
Daniels. The man asked John how it went with
Yayo. John asked him who that was. The man
told him it was the man who sold him that
sweet young thing.

"Oh yeah. Are there more around?" John
asked him.

"Hold on a second."

He goes into the back, and grabs the younger guy, Sammy, telling John that Sammy will take him to the girls. The boy seemed nervous, awkward. They walked out of the store. John wasn't even charged for the Jack or the Coke. The boy's eyes darted. He was edgy. John asked Sammy how many girls there were, but didn't answer. John held his gun in his pocket. They took a shortcut and started jogging down an alley that was clearly not a shortcut to the hotel. John followed cautiously. The boy awkwardly stopped in the middle of the alley, and pulled a Colt .45. John pulled his Special from his pocket, and shot the boy in the head. Works every time. Sammy's eyes went blank, portions of his brain stuck to the wooden privacy fence. John ran.

Jimmy had been to the house. He left John a message that read 'Meet me at my old house. It's about Alexandra." John grabbed it, wadded it up, and trashed it. He put another bullet in his pistol, drank a glass of orange juice, and left, running, moving with purpose.

Adam was doctoring a gouge in Jimmy's arm. It looked like it needed stitches. John rang the doorbell. Adam ran down, run down, but alert.

"Hey. Jimmy thinks he knows where his sister and my fiancé are being kept."
"Yeah?"
"Come on in."

"We should call the police." John said.

"I have. It's no use."

"Yeah," Jimmy said, "We can just go there, get the girls out. The kidnappers aren't so big. I can take 'em!"

"Kidnappers?" John asked.

Jimmy told John that there were two kidnappers. They were skinny and out of shape. John asked Jimmy where he saw Alexandra, how he saw Alexandra.

"I didn't mean to, really. I was just walking down the street, and I heard a man scream. He stumbled out onto his front lawn and collapsed, stab wounds all over him. He was totally bloody. I think he died, but a girl wearing Alexandra's shirt and a black fur coat came out. She dropped a knife on the front porch and I think she saw me, but I'm not sure, but I got scared, and then I ran into a bush behind someone's house. She didn't seem to wanna chase me. I don't know why. I followed her and she went about six blocks, past Grand River. Other girls went up to her, all really young and walking at the same slow pace. It was really creepy. They went to this house and through the side door. A blue minivan pulled in, and more girls got out. They all went to the basement. I went to the side to look in, but all the windows were painted white. I just heard noises. A few were from the backyard, under the porch. There was a girl wearing a muzzle, tied up. I undid it and she told me I had to get her out of there. She'd been tied up for three weeks, fed only mayonnaise and Crisco, which she had to eat from a doggy bowl. The garage opened and we both got really scared. We ran in opposite directions. I didn't look back. I don't know if she's okay, but I think I know where Alexandra and Jen are!"

"Who's Jen?"

"My fiancé?" Adam interrupts, "Got kidnapped last night? John, they took her right from this table, right in front of me. We were drugged. They drugged my food, in my house! They must have done it while I was picking her up at the airport. I woke up, and she was gone."

"Well we definitely need help," John said.

"Look, man. The police aren't responding. Those mad men could be torturing those girls.

We need to act and we need to act now."

"I brought daddy's gun!" Jimmy said excitedly.

John snatched the gun from Jimmy and handed it to Adam. Jimmy complained that he needed a weapon. Adam gave him the mace.

Jimmy didn't want pepper-spray. It was what he was stuck with. They ran to Grand River.

THIRTEEN

The girls had lined up in Rufus'
basement, later than normal. John, Jimmy, and
Adam approached the house. John told the
boys to split up. Jimmy didn't want to be
alone. John made him, but the second John
was out of sight, Jimmy ran to Adam, and
acted as lookout for whomever came out of
the garage. On the other side of the house,
John found a scratch in the painted window.
He could see a militaristic line of girls,
perfectly parallel to the walls. He saw Rufus
holding a gray bucket. One of the girls read
from a book; it looked to be a Bible. Rufus
pulled a man's heart from the bucket, and held
it up. The girls' heads acted as one, eyes
adjusting to their fleshy god. Rufus yelled at

the girl with the book. He snatched it from her, shoved the heart in her mouth. She took a bite, and passed it down the line. He pulled a liver from the bucket, and repeated with another girl who took her bite and passed it down the line. The girls ate without hesitation in a ritualistic feeding frenzy, too smooth to be human anymore.

John spotted Alexandra, as she broke the stern, relentless conformity of her peers. Rufus held up a male's genitals from the bucket and she kneeled, wanting to take the first bite out of the dead, pale, flaccid penis. Rufus slapped her in the face with it. Dusty mixed chemicals in the corner, but ran up to Rufus to stop him from beating Alexandra.

Rufus started to beat Dusty with the bloodied cock. Dusty took it. Rufus looked at the window, saw John's silhouette cast onto it, lit by a streetlight. Dusty was happy, he wanted the man outside to win, but then he got sad. Who'd take care of him? Would he be eating out of trashcans again, fighting over food with strays in alleys? Rufus gave him a better life. He cleaned him up, he gave him purpose, he allowed him to be around all the beautiful girls and make them the most beautiful in the world. Dusty couldn't let that life end.

He grabbed the crossbow on the wall, aimed it at John's head. The bolt flew sluggishly, yet fast, and very heavy. It busted the window, and flew into John's leg. The sound of thick glass breaking and John's screams echoed throughout the entire neighborhood. Jimmy and Adam felt the thrash from the driveway. Jimmy saw a chain, taut, four feet off the ground, suspended between the garage and the side of the house. He pulled it. It wiggled, and dropped limp onto the back lawn. A large figure, dark, unknowable, wore a leash, carrying John over his shoulder and into the garage through the side door. Uncle John screamed for help. Clearly, then muffled.

"Jimmy! Get the damn mace ready!" Adam yelled.

A large fishing net, weighed down by lead on the sides fell off the roof and onto Adam. Dusty ran out, Jimmy was mortified and couldn't squeeze the trigger on the mace. The fear was a shot of adrenaline. Without looking at Dusty, Jimmy shot the mace in his face. Dusty started screaming, crying, drooling, mumbling. He staggered, and almost collapsed onto Jimmy, but his head smacked the garage door. He lost his balance, and twisted his ankle, falling, like an oaf, hard onto the driveway.

A strong smoky smell filled the air. The air became foggy, thick, and moist. The air burned. As the smoke died down, the man on the leash emerged from the garage. Jimmy was crouching behind the van. Dusty banged on the garage, crying and on his knees. He screamed for J.J. The light inside illuminated the man on the leash, J.J., as he made his way through the murky smoke. Jimmy tried to find his way to his Uncle or to Adam. As the smoke began to die down, Jimmy saw that J.J. walked slowly, an axe in his back. J.J. mumbled something foreign. John grabbed the leash, swung it around J.J's neck, and yanked hard. J.J. fell onto a steel workbench within a minute, slamming his head on a tabletop before plummeting to the cold, cemented ground. John kneelt down and snapped the guy's neck. Just in case.

The side door opened violently and out came Rufus, running, running hard. He gave a quick gaze at J.J's dead body. He reanimated, sending shivers, fear, and hopelessness down John, Adam, and Jimmy's spines. Rufus understood what he was up against, but appeared magical and apathetic. Adam pointed the gun at Rufus, and pulled the trigger as the gun mystically turned on himself. The bullet nicked his shoulder. The force thrust Adam towards Rufus, who tried to steal the gun away from him. Adam had a firm grip. They struggled. Thinking of Jen, he found the power to win the fight, when Rufus sunk his teeth into Adam's Adam's apple.

John was locked in battle with the reanimated J.J. Jimmy's grip was sweaty, tightly clenching the mace, but feared getting it on Adam or John. The muzzled girl reappeared behind J.J. With a cordless power drill, she wound the bit into his spine, causing him to shriek his final cry of death that echoed to the depths of Hell and back. Blood spurted out of every orifice, dark and pungent with a rotten smell to match. The girl began to vomit, but the muzzle forced her to choke. John got the muzzle off. Puke projected from her mouth for five feet.

Rufus watched as if he had gotten sucked into one of his horror flicks, laughing at the cartoonish display. Jimmy glanced at his uncle, and then back at Rufus, who was staring him down. Adam was wrestling with Rufus again, but Rufus just treated it like a game. Jimmy felt Rufus enter his mind and began to walk over to the J.J.'s corpse. He wanted to grab the axe. He wanted to hack his Uncle John into pieces. He snapped out of it, terrified at what nearly happened and ran to Rufus to kick him in the nuts as hard as he could. He just kept kicking and kicking. Adam finally got Rufus in a hold.

Rufus smiled as he leaned towards the ground. Jimmy was more frightened than ever. A gunshot erupted. Dusty had gotten Uncle John's gun. John was on his knees.

"Na-na-na-now you la-la-la-let g-go uh-uh-of that m-man a-and p-p-p-put y-your hands up and c-c-c-come o-over here, r-right now!" Dusty stammered.

Adam let go. Rufus fell to his knees. Jimmy put his hands up, and walked towards Dusty and his uncle. Dusty lined the three men up. Jimmy took a hard look at Rufus who was mentally orchestrating their execution. Rufus kept trying to control Jimmy, but Jimmy resisted. Dusty seemed too calm as Jimmy stood up and ran to the axe. Dusty twisted, his body and pointed the gun at Jimmy's head. As he pulled the trigger, Adam shot Dusty in the head. A bullet whizzed past Jimmy's head. Realizing he wasn't dead Jimmy concluded that Rufus controlled Dusty through telepathy like he'd been trying to do to him. John collapsed. He'd lost a lot of blood. Jimmy wanted to grab the gun and shoot Rufus, but he wasn't there. Adam was running. Jimmy grabbed the gun and ran to the front yard where a large black dog pranced away, gracefully turning its head, gazing at Adam and Jimmy with its demonic eyes.

Jimmy felt sick, the same violent thoughts entered his mind, but this time it was to shoot Adam in the head. Again, he resisted. The dog galloped into the darkness. The police and an ambulance showed up, alerted by the gunshots. The EMS tech rushed John onto a stretcher, and into the ambulance before driving off. The police went into the house. One man ran upstairs, another downstairs. The girls had disappeared. Adam and Jimmy weren't allowed in. They were told that there was no one in the house. Adam told them that that was impossible. They forced their way in anyways. The cops didn't really care. There was a cry from above. Jimmy saw a string from the ceiling. It led to the attic. They pulled down the stairs and there were the girls, done up and ready for the night's work. It was a clean room, and in the corner were Charlene's voodoo doll of Rufus and nineteen Barbie dolls made to resemble the girls, facing the Rufus doll. Nineteen candles were placed on the sides.

The police led the girls down the stairs. They remained unresponsive and in a line, cattle being led to slaughter, only they were saved from their turmoil. The sergeant tells one of the younger officers to bag the dolls as evidence. He goes back to the attic and finds the Rufus doll gone. In its place was a statue of the black dog. The girls faced the dog now.

Ten minutes pass. The girls are standing despondently in the driveway. There is a gunshot. They laugh in a choir, while staring at the attic. A pair of officers rush back upstairs. The officer shot himself in the head and most of his brains landed at the feet of the black dog. The dolls smiled.

Made in the USA
Lexington, KY
19 April 2012